Welcome to ALADDIN QUIX!

If you are looking for fast, fun-to-read stories with colorful characters, lots of kid-friendly humor, easy-to-follow action, entertaining story lines, and lively illustrations, then **ALADDIN QUIX** is for you!

But wait, there's more!

If you're also looking for stories with tables of contents; word lists; about-the-book questions; 64, 80, or 96 pages; short chapters; short paragraphs; and large fonts, then **ALADDIN QUIX** is *definitely* for you!

ALADDIN QUIX: The next step between ready to reads and longer, more challenging chapter books, for readers five to eight years old.

Read more ALADDIN QUIX books!

By Stephanie Calmenson

Our Principal Is a Frog!

Our Principal Is a Wolf!

Our Principal's in His Underwear!

Our Principal Breaks a Spell!

Our Principal's Wacky Wishes!

Our Principal Is a Spider!

The Adventures of Allie and Amy
By Stephanie Calmenson and Joanna Cole

The Best Friend Plan

Rockin' Rockets

Stars of the Show

Our Principal Is a Scaredy-Cat!

ᴮʸ Stephanie Calmenson

ɪʟʟᴜꜱᴛʀᴀᴛᴇᴅ ʙʏ Aaron Blecha

ALADDIN QUIX

New York London Toronto Sydney New Delhi

To Emily and Joshua, with love
—S. C.

ALADDIN QUIX
Simon & Schuster Children's Publishing Division
1230 Avenue of the Americas, New York, New York 10020
First Aladdin QUIX hardcover edition May 2021
Text copyright © 2021 by Stephanie Calmenson
Illustrations copyright © 2021 by Aaron Blecha
Also available in an Aladdin QUIX paperback edition.
All rights reserved, including the right of reproduction in whole or in part in any form.
ALADDIN and the related marks and colophon are
trademarks of Simon & Schuster, Inc.
For information about special discounts for bulk purchases, please contact
Simon & Schuster Special Sales at 1-866-506-1949 or business@simonandschuster.com.
The Simon & Schuster Speakers Bureau can bring authors to your live event. For
more information or to book an event contact the Simon & Schuster Speakers Bureau
at 1-866-248-3049 or visit our website at www.simonspeakers.com.
Designed by Karin Paprocki
The illustrations for this book were rendered digitally.
The text of this book was set in Archer Medium.
Manufactured in the United States of America 0421 LAK
2 4 6 8 10 9 7 5 3 1
Library of Congress Control Number 2020951309
ISBN 9781534479357 (hc)
ISBN 9781534479340 (pbk)
ISBN 9781534479364 (ebook)

Cast of Characters

Mr. Barnaby Bundy: Principal

Roger Patel: Top student and class leader

Nancy Wong: Plans to be a zoologist

Hector Gonzalez: Loves making his friends laugh

Ms. Marilyn Moore: Assistant principal

Ms. Karen Cole: School nurse

Alice Wright: Kindergarten student

Ms. Ellie Tilly: Kindergarten teacher

Keesha Johnson: Star athlete

Mr. Nate Langer: Music teacher

Ms. Stella Abbott: Cafeteria worker

Marty Q. Marvel: Bumbling magician

Contents

Our Principal
Is a Scaredy-Cat!

1

A Spiffy Hat

Principal Bundy was riding his bike to school early Monday morning when he suddenly hit a bump in the road.

Hissss. Air was leaking out of his back tire. When he got off his bike to look, the tire was completely flat.

This is why I leave extra time to get to school, he thought.

He took out his tool kit, patched the hole, pumped air into the tire, and was ready to go.

While he was picking up his pump, he noticed a **spiffy** hat on the ground.

If I clean up this hat, I'm sure it will look quite nice on me, thought Mr. Bundy, who enjoyed dressing well.

He stuffed the hat into his jacket pocket and continued on his way to school. He still had plenty of time to get there and then greet his students, which was a favorite part of his morning.

As he waited by the school door, he saw **Roger**, **Nancy**, and **Hector** coming his way. It was almost Halloween, and Hector was telling a Dracula joke.

"What kind of dog does Dracula have?" said Hector.

"I believe Count Dracula has

the very rare Transylvanian Bat Beagle," said Roger, who was one of the top students in his class.

"You made that up! There's no such kind," said Nancy, whose hobby was studying animals.

"If the two of you are finished, I'll tell you the answer," said Hector. **"Dracula has a bloodhound!"**

"Grrr," said Nancy.

"We can always *count* on you for a goofy joke," said Roger. "Get it? Count? Count Dracula?"

"Grrr," said Hector.

"Morning, kids," said Mr. Bundy cheerfully.

"Morning, Mr. B!" they called.

The kids joked and growled their way through the door. When the last student was inside the building, Mr. Bundy went to his office and hung his jacket in the closet. He was ready for another exciting PS 88 day.

2

Who Said That?

"Knock, knock!" said **Ms. Moore,** the assistant principal. She poked her head into Mr. Bundy's office and waved a paper in the air. "I brought

everyone's **schedule** for the Fall
Fun Festival."

"Let's see what we've got," said
Mr. Bundy, checking the list.

- ✔ Halloween Song
- ✔ Pumpkin Parade
- ✔ Autumn Leaf Poems
- ✔ Scarecrow Shuffle

"This looks great, thanks," said
Mr. Bundy.

When Ms. Moore left, the

principal turned on the microphone for his morning greeting.

"Good morning, PS 88! I've just received your Fall Fun Festival ideas and am glad to see a nice mix of—"

Out of nowhere, Mr. Bundy heard a voice whisper, *"Give it back."*

He looked around. There was no one in the office but him. He assumed the voice had come from outside, and continued speaking.

"As I was saying, I'm glad to see a nice mix of programs,

from fall harvest celebrations to

Halloween fun and—"

"Give it back!" said the

voice.

Mr. Bundy turned toward the door. No one had come in. He glanced out the window. No one was passing by.

He wondered if a student might be playing a trick on him. **No way!** His students loved him and would never do such a thing.

While he was wondering where the voice might be coming from, he heard it again, this time a little louder.

Something really weird is

going on, thought Mr. Bundy.

He wanted to wrap up his announcement quickly before the voice got loud enough for anyone else to hear. He spoke as fast as he could, trying not to trip over his tongue.

"I'm-looking-forward-to-Friday's-Fall-Fun-Festival-and-wish-you-all-a-fine-and-friendly-fall-day!"

He turned off the microphone just before the voice, even louder than before, said, **"Give it back!"**

Mr. Bundy looked up, down, and around. There was still no one in the office except for him. In a moment there would be no one at all because he was way too scared to stay.

He leaped up, ran out, and quickly shut the door behind him.

3

Say "Ahhh"

In the hallway, Mr. Bundy saw **Ms. Cole**, the school nurse, coming his way.

"Are you okay, Mr. Bundy? You look as though you've seen a ghost," she said.

"I'm fine," said Mr. Bundy.

What he was really thinking was, *I didn't see a ghost, but I may have* heard *one.*

"You don't look fine. You look **feverish**. Follow me, please," said Ms. Cole.

"Oh no, no, no," said Mr. Bundy. "Really, I'm fine."

"Oh yes, yes, yes," said the nurse. "Really, you are not. Follow me."

When they got to her office,

Ms. Cole took out a **tongue depressor**.

"Open wide and say, 'Ahhh,'" she told the principal.

Mr. Bundy's shoulders **slumped**.

"Do I have to?" he said. "Those things make me gag."

"Yes, you have to," said Ms. Cole. "Open wide."

"Ahhh, ahhh, aargh!" said Mr. Bundy.

"Your throat looks clear," said Ms. Cole.

Just then, **Alice** from **Ms. Tilly**'s class came in.

"May I please have a Band-Aid?" she asked. "I just cut my pinkie."

Then she saw the principal and said, **"Hi, Mr. Bundy!"**

"Alice, I need you to wait," said Ms. Cole. "I'll get you a Band-Aid in a moment."

The nurse turned back to the principal and put a thermometer in his ear.

"Hee-hee, that tickles!" said Mr. Bundy.

"Stay still, please," said Ms. Cole.

"Do I have to?" asked Mr. Bundy.

"Yes, you have to," said Alice

before the nurse could answer. "Be brave, Mr. B."

Mr. Bundy listened to Alice and stayed still until he heard the thermometer beep.

"You don't have a fever," said Ms. Cole.

Next she put a **stethoscope** on Mr. Bundy's chest so she could listen to his heart.

"Eeek!" yipped Mr. Bundy. "That's cold."

"You're not behaving very well," said Alice.

"It's okay," said Ms. Cole. "We're done now. Mr. Bundy, I think you've been working too hard. You need to eat well, exercise, and rest."

And I need to stop hearing voices in empty rooms, thought Mr. Bundy.

But what he said was, "Thank you, Ms. Cole. I'll do my best." Then he turned to Alice and said, "I know you will be a very good patient, and I hope your pinkie will be better soon."

4

Gotta Run!

Mr. Bundy straightened his tie and returned to his office feeling quite a bit **calmer**.

Nurse Cole is right, he thought. *I've been working too hard. I'm probably just imagining things.*

But when he opened the door to his office, he heard: **"Give me . . ."**

He shut the door fast, waited a moment, then opened it just a crack.

The voice went, **"Tee-hee-hee!"** as if this were a funny game.

Mr. Bundy quickly shut the door. As soon as he opened it again, he heard, **"Nyah, nyah!"** And he shut it once more.

"This silliness must stop!" said Mr. Bundy, shaking his finger at the door.

He did not hear Nancy and her classmate **Keesha** coming down the hall on a bathroom break. Seeing their principal **scolding** a door, they held in their giggles and quietly backed away.

Mr. Bundy was not going to open that door again anytime soon. He walked away from his office, trying to decide what to do.

He considered telling Ms. Moore,

then decided against it. She'd never believe him. Who would?

Not knowing where to go next, he walked through the halls, admiring all the **impressive** dis-

plays. There were paper cut-
outs of bright autumn leaves,
and Halloween storybooks with
ghosts and goblins jumping
from the pages.

When Mr. Bundy heard singing coming from the music room, he stopped to listen.

"Welcome! Please come join us," said **Mr. Langer**, the music teacher. "Mrs. Feeny's class is practicing their song for the fall festival." He turned to the class and said, "Let's start from the beginning and do a great job for Mr. Bundy."

The kids sang loudly with lots of spooky spirit for their principal.

*"Have you seen
the ghost of John?
Long white bones
and the rest all gone!
Oooh-oooh! Oooh-oooh!
Oooh-oooh-oooh!
Wouldn't it be chilly
with no skin on?"*

Oooh, oooh, oooh! Poor Mr. Bundy! He was not happy hearing such a **shivery** song about a skeleton.

Seeing him turn ghostly pale,

Mr. Langer held up his hand to stop the singing.

"Great song. Gotta run. **Goodbye!**" said Mr. Bundy.

And he was gone in a flash.

5

Conga!

Mr. Bundy was still too scared to return to his office. Instead he **wandered** from classroom to classroom and was a welcome visitor wherever he went.

When he stopped by Ms. Tilly's

kindergarten, Alice was in front of the room about to make a presentation.

"Look, Mr. Bundy! I got a Band-Aid with pumpkins on it," she said, waving her pinkie.

"Why don't you read your poem now?" said Ms. Tilly. "I'm sure Mr. Bundy would like to hear it."

"I certainly would," said Mr. Bundy.

"I wrote this by myself and it rhymes," said Alice. Then she began to recite.

"See autumn leaves
on the ground.
See them swirling
round and round.
They're lining up
for the conga dance.
Join them now
if you get the chance.
Soon the leaves
will blow away.
If you like my poem,
please shout
'Hooray!'"

"**Hooray!**" called Mr. Bundy, along with the rest of the class.

Alice took her bows as everyone clapped.

"On your feet," said Ms. Tilly. **"Let's all do the conga!"**

The class lined up, then danced round and round the room, singing a conga song.

"Round the room we conga!
In a line we conga!
We love to do the conga!
Everybody, conga!"

Mr. Bundy, who had joined the end of the line, swung off when he got to the door. "Thank you so much, Alice. Your autumn poem is just what I needed," he said.

6

Sloppy Joe

The principal felt much better after his visit with Ms. Tilly's class.

Walking with a spring in his step, he decided there had to be a completely reasonable explanation for the voice he'd been hearing.

After stopping by a few more classrooms, the principal joined the children for lunch in the cafeteria. Wanting no special treatment, he took his place in line.

"What a nice surprise, Mr. Bundy!" said **Ms. Abbott,** who was serving lunch. "What can I get you from the special fall menu?"

"The turkey-lurky sloppy joe's really good, Mr. B," said Hector, who was next in line.

"**Excellent!** That's what I'll have," said Mr. Bundy.

"One turkey-lurky sloppy joe coming right up. It's my very own recipe," said Ms. Abbott, serving up a generous **portion**.

"Thank you. It looks delicious," said Mr. Bundy.

As he was walking away with his lunch, he suddenly heard a voice shout, **"Give it back!"**

Mr. Bundy stopped short. His hands began to shake. By the time he realized the voice had

come from a student arguing
over a candy bar, half his sloppy
joe had spilled onto his lunch
tray.

"Are you all right, Mr. Bundy?"

asked Ms. Abbott. "Can I get you a fresh serving?"

"No, no, I'm fine. I ... um ... just tripped over my own feet," said Mr. Bundy.

Thanks to the scare, the principal had lost his **appetite**. He didn't want to **insult** Ms. Abbott by not eating her food, so he gobbled down his very sloppy sloppy joe. Then he left the cafeteria and wandered from room to room till the end of the day.

Finally, when everyone was gone

from school, he couldn't put off returning to his office any longer. It was time to get his jacket and go home. With fear in his heart he walked slowly down the hall.

Then he got an idea.

7

Ring-Ring!

Instead of going to his own office, Mr. Bundy went to Ms. Moore's office and made a phone call.

Ring-ring! Ring-ring!

He was greatly **relieved** when his call was answered.

"**Marty Q. Marvel** here! My marvelous magic will amaze you!" said the magician's familiar voice.

Marty Q. Marvel had visited PS 88 on several occasions. The truth was that his magic really wasn't marvelous. His tricks either didn't work at all or went **haywire**.

One time he turned Mr. Bundy into a frog, then forgot how to reverse the spell. It took a happy accident to turn Mr. Bundy back into a person.

But if there was anyone who would believe the strange goings-on of the day, it was Marty.

Whether or not Marty's magic worked, Mr. Bundy would be glad to have his company. He did not want to go back into his office alone.

"If you're not busy right now, could you please come over?" said the principal. "I'm having a little problem here at school, and I hope you can help me."

"I'll be there in a **jiffy**!" said the magician.

In no time, he came tripping through the door.

"*Whoops!* Marty Q. Marvel at your service!" he said. "How can I help?"

Mr. Bundy led Marty to his office. While standing outside, he explained his problem. The principal had to talk louder and louder because the magician was slowly backing farther and farther away.

"Where are you going?" asked Mr. Bundy.

"I'm a big scaredy-cat!" Marty called from down the hall. "There's no way I'm going in. I'll try a magic spell from here." Then he began:

"And a-one! And a-two!
And a-one, two, three!
Be gone scary voice.
I set you free!"

Mr. Bundy put his ear to the door. All was quiet.

He opened the door a crack. Still quiet.

He waited a moment more. When there wasn't a sound, he opened the door wide and breathed a sigh of relief.

"It worked! Your magic

really *is* amazing," said Mr. Bundy. "Come in while I get my jacket, and we'll walk out together."

Marty inched toward the office. When all was still quiet, he followed Mr. Bundy inside. He felt very proud. He also felt very surprised, since he wasn't used to having his magic work.

But a moment later . . .

8

Scaredy-Cats

"*Give it back!*" said the voice.

Marty jumped up onto Mr. Bundy's desk. He really *was* a scaredy-cat, just as he'd said. Mr. Bundy was scaredy-cat number two, jumping right up with him.

"What do we do now?" said Marty, trembling.

"You've got to try another magic spell!" said Mr. Bundy.

"And a—! And a—! And-I'm-a too scared!" said Marty.

That's when the voice roared louder than ever,

"GIVE IT BACK!"

That did it! The voice scared the scaredy-cats into answering. At the very same time, they closed their eyes tight and shouted together:

"TAKE IT!!!"

Their eyes were still shut when they heard a rattling sound, like the rattling of bones. They heard Mr. Bundy's closet door creak open, then creak closed.

It took a long time for Mr. Bundy and Marty to open their eyes and come down from the desk. When they finally did, Marty said, "We don't have to tell anyone what just happened, do we?"

"We definitely do not. This will be our little secret," said Mr. Bundy. The principal grabbed his jacket from the closet. Then the two scaredy-cats left the school together. They were happy to be rid of whatever they'd just heard.

That evening while emptying his jacket pockets, Mr. Bundy remembered the spiffy hat he'd found that morning. He was surprised that it was gone.

It must have fallen out on my

ride home, he thought. *Maybe I'll find it on my way back to school tomorrow.*

He didn't find the hat the next day. Or the next. Or the next.

By Friday, Mr. Bundy was ready to enjoy the Fall Fun Festival. He had invited Marty, who was sitting in the front row.

Everyone at school cheered at the Pumpkin Parade and tapped their toes to the Scarecrow Shuffle.

Wearing a costume of bright fall leaves, Alice **recited** her poem.

When she finished, everyone shouted **"Hooray!"**

Next Mrs. Feeny's class danced

out dressed as skeletons and began to sing their Halloween song.

They sang loudly with lots of spooky spirit, just as they'd practiced.

*"Have you seen
the ghost of John?
Long white bones
and the rest all gone!"*

With everyone's eyes on the singers, no one noticed the skeleton looking in at the window. No one heard his bones rattling as he danced to the music.

No one noticed except poor Mr. Bundy, who tried to be

brave when he saw the grinning skeleton wink at him and tip his spiffy hat.

Oooh-oooh! Oooh-oooh-oooh!

Word List

appetite (A•puh•tite): The desire to eat

calmer (KAHL•mur): More relaxed

feverish (FEE•vur•ish): Having a high body temperature

haywire (HAY•wire): Being out of order or not working properly

impressive (ihm•PREH•siv): Having the power to attract attention or admiration

insult (in•SUHLT): To treat rudely

jiffy (JIH•fee): A very short amount of time

portion (POR•shun): A part of the whole

recited (rih•SIGH•ted): Repeated from memory or read aloud

relieved (rih•LEEVD): Feeling or showing relief

schedule (SKEH•jool): A plan of things to be done at certain times

scolding (SKOHLD•ing):
Speaking to angrily for bad
behavior

shivery (SHIH•vuh•ree): Causing
shaking out of fear or cold

slumped (SLUHMPT): Fell or
sank suddenly

spiffy (SPIH•fee): Fine looking

stethoscope (STEH•thuh•skope):
A medical instrument used to
listen to a person's heart or lungs

**tongue depressor (TUHNG
dih•PREH•sur):** A thin, flat piece
of wood rounded at both ends,

used to press down on a person's
tongue to give a better view of
the throat

wandered (WAHN•derd):
Walked around with no clear
reason or direction

Questions

1. Can you remember the last time you felt like a scaredy-cat? Would the same thing scare you now?

2. Next time you get scared, will you call Marty Q. Marvel? If not, whom will you call?

3. If your school were having a Fall Fun Festival, what activity would you choose to do?

4. There are folktales told all around the world in which an

animal or ghostly spirit loses something and wants it back. If you were a ghostly spirit, who—or what!—would you be? What would you lose and want back?

5. Do you know a Halloween song? If you do, sing it out loud with spooky spirit.

FAST★FUN★READS

LOOKING FOR A FAST, FUN READ? BE SURE TO MAKE IT ALADDIN QUIX!

EBOOK EDITIONS ALSO AVAILABLE

ALADDIN QUIX • SIMONANDSCHUSTER.COM/KIDS

CHUCKLE YOUR WAY THROUGH THESE EASY-TO-READ ILLUSTRATED CHAPTER BOOKS!

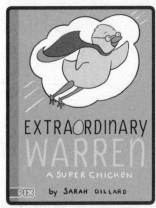

EBOOK EDITIONS ALSO AVAILABLE